Hello,

Sharing this book with the youth of the world brings us one step closer to reclaiming our innocents and building a generation of children who will be well equipped to make the world a more connected and desirable place to be. It is not a secret that the youth of today is being exposed to a world of technology that has shifted their communication, physical, and interpersonal skills. As parents, educators, family members, and friends it is up to us to incorporate and expose the youth to a balanced lifestyle. With the lessons of "The Gobster," we can begin to address the imbalance that currently is eroding the minds of the young ones we love. Let's bring balance back into their lives and say goodbye to the Gobster in all of us.

I am a teacher, a nutritionist, an author, an artist, a daughter, a family member, a friend, parent, and now I am partner and committed with you to bring about balance, health, and nutrition into the lives of the young people of this world. Thank you for buying this book and bringing us one step closer to addressing the issue of our children overindulging in modern technology. Visit, www.TheGobster.com for more information.

Best Wishes,
Nicole Roach

The Gobster
Adventures of Ace

Author, Nicole Roach
Illustrator, Valerie Cody

In the morning Ace awakes,
To the smell of mother's fresh pancakes.
With one great leap he's on his feet
Now he heads to his breakfast seat.
He's through the hall and down the stairs
When he is stopped by a familiar glare

He's captivated by the attractive glow
Of his favorite morning T.V. show.
It isn't too long before his eyes begin to ache
And he forgets about Mom's sweet pancakes.

Feeling tired and sluggish from his shows
Ace struggles to put on his new school clothes.
Looking at the clock, Ace knows he's late
But mother's breakfast is still on his plate!
He grabs a handful of food to eat
And rushes to the bus stop where all the kids meet.

Now sitting on the bus he is surrounded by his friends
But on his headphones is where all his attention ends
Ace's friends reach out to him more and more
But his biggest concern is his next high score.

Aces' buddies let him know,
As any good friend would,
That they miss a lot
But he didn't miss them as he should.

Now, sitting in class,
His teacher is concerned -
"Where is your homework?
I need to know you've learned."
Sadly, he replies:
"I'm sorry Mrs. Nye;
But it's hard to tell you a lie."
And with a somber sigh he says,
"I really didn't even try."

Feeling pretty low,
He starts feeling even lower.
A belly ache and a chill,
And so many questions still.

He's trying to remember,
Where all his time goes.
But all he can think of is
Video games and TV shows.

The school bell rings
And all the children sing,
"Our school day is done!"
But Ace isn't having fun.

Tired and feeling like a slouch
All he can think of is his games
And his couch
Then he thinks to himself,
"I know just the trick
I'll play video games
Until I don't feel sick."

Ace asks for a cookie,
As he tosses his books on the floor.
Then he grabs his controller
And plays games until his thumbs are sore.

His thumbs are throbbing,
His stomach is turning,
Even his eyes are burning!
And through all the pain,
He keeps playing his game.

But when Ace is finally done playing his game,
He suddenly realizes -
He still feels the same!

Soon, he feels even worse than before.
Upstairs in his room, he shuts the door
He turns on his computer once more.
To internet, music, and even more games
Ace feels like he has to explore.

"It's time for dinner," his mother calls out.
"And be sure to wash up before I have to shout!"

Washing his hands, Ace looks up
And what he saw was a surprise
His own reflection catches his eye.
His eyes well up and he starts to cry.
He can't see himself, as hard as he tries!

With tears down his cheeks,
It's his mother he seeks.
He cries out to his Mom,
"What is happening to me?
My eyes are so heavy
I can barely see!
All of my fingers are bent,
My energy's spent,
My arms look like spaghetti and meatballs
And I feel so big I'm not sure I can get through the halls.
My face is slimy and covered in goo - "
Ace looks in the mirror and shouts, "EW!"
"My hair is so wiry, it's too tough to comb through!
Mom, look at my belly,
It looks like some weird jelly.
What is happening to me?
Oh, WHAT'S HAPPENING TO ME?"

With great sympathy his mom sighs,
"I can hardly believe my eyes!
I've seen something like this before,
with Misty, the little girl next door.
I bet the reasons are the same.
She lost herself in TV, music, and video games.
And all that junk food - what a shame!
You'll look like this every day
Unless you change your ways
You better shape up Ace
Or you will turn into a Gobster"

Fear is growing in his teary eyes,
"Gobster, what's that?" he cries.
And Ace's Mom replies,
"A Gobster is what anyone becomes
If they sit too long on their bums.
It happens to girls and boys
That play with too many toys,
Or stay inside all day
And waste away.
They don't eat right
And turn into a Gobster overnight."

Tears are streaming from his eyes,
Ace slouches and he sighs,
"What should I do?
Am I a Gobster too?"

Clutching him in her arms, Ace's mom replies,
"Ace my love, don't feel too blue.
You can find your way back to you!
Just listen to me and you'll be okay.
Get up early on every school day,
So you can eat right and fill your tummy
And not end up feeling weak and gummy.

You'll finish your homework faster, too,
And Mrs. Nye will be so very proud of you!
After school, don't sit on your bum
Go outside with your friends and have lots of fun!

With a look of fear, Ace cries, "I don't know how!"

Kids can sometimes be so cruel.
How can I face them and go back to school?
Won't I look such a fool?

You tell me to be strong -
But Mom, what if you're wrong?"

To that, Ace's mom just smiled a lot
And said, "My dear; I know I'm not."

While walking to school the next day
Ace felt pretty darn grey.
He said "what's up" to his friends
And to his surprise they smiled and said, "Hey."

He's feeling a little better
And he begins to smile
When he realizes he can see his face
So he jokes and laughs with his friends,
Like one big warm embrace.

His teacher said, "It's good to see you smile with your friends again,
Instead of a Gobster who wasn't anyone's friend."

Feeling full of energy,
He follows his friends
To their favorite tree.
He climbs the branches
And feels the breeze.

After lunch, it's time for class.
He participates, and joyfully he smiles
When his paper says he passed.

Feeling stronger than ever,
Now happy and more clever,
The time came when he realized
He could see clearly from both eyes!
His fingers were not bloated
And his skin wasn't oil-coated.

When Ace got home, he burst through the door,
And shouted to his mom, "I'm not a Gobster anymore!"
Mom smiled and hugged him and said,
"Now, that's my boy. Way to use your head."

Later that night while lying in bed, Ace looks up to the sky
Anticipating all the new things he might try.
His mom tucks him in and kisses him good night
And tells him she's proud that he's doing things right.

Softly she says, "Close your eyes, it's time for rest,
so that tomorrow you can be at your very best."

THE GOBSTER QUIZ TAKE THIS SURVEY AND FIND OUT IF YOU'RE A GOBSTER.

1. When you get home from school or a long day you:
    - A. Grab a book and sit down and read it
    - B. Watch TV
    - C. Go straight to your bedroom
    - D. Play video games

1. When you go on a road trip what is your favorite item to bring?
    - A. Mad Libs
    - B. Note pad and pen
    - C. Movies
    - D. Head Phones and music

1. Your family and you are going to a restaurant that you go to often you:
    - A. Play your hand held video game
    - B. Draw on your napkin
    - C. Talk with your family
    - D. Complain that you'd rather be home

1. You have some play time at home, your preferred activity is:
    - A. Playing on the internet
    - B. Playing baseball or other outdoor games with your friends
    - C. Texting on your phone
    - D. Pretend you're a pirate and look for treasure around the house

1. While your in class you:
    - A. Fall asleep
    - B. Ask questions to the teacher
    - C. Toss paper balls around
    - D. Talk to your friends

Answers:

1. A- 0 B-2 C-1 D-3
2. A- 0 B-1 C-2 D-3
3. A-3 B-1 C-0 D-2
4. A- 3 B-0 C-2 D-1
5. A-3 B-0 C-2 D-1

If you scored:
1-5 You are not a Gobster
6-11 You are in danger of turning into a Gobster
12-15 You are a Gobster

THE GOBSTER JOURNAL QUESTIONS

Gobster Journal

We all have a little Gobster inside of us and here is your chance to discover the Gobster inside yourself. Take a few moments and discuss these questions. Use the journal pages to write down your answers, questions, and ideas.

Questions to discuss:

1. How am I like a Gobster?

2. What can I do to make sure I don't turn into a Gobster?

3. If I could do anything with my day what would I do?

4. Do I know anyone who most resembles a Gobster?
   In your opinion, how do this person resembles a Gobster?

5. What can my parents do to support my efforts?

Lines for the answers to the journal questions.

_____

_____

_____

_____

_____

_____

_____

_____

_____

_____

_____

_____

_____

_____

Made in the USA
San Bernardino, CA
11 April 2019